I dedicate this book to
Mother Earth for all her
thought and consideration
for every living thing.

www.mascotbooks.com

Wiggly Worm and Her Friends Recycle Organics

For more information, please contact:
Mascot Books
620 Herndon Parkway, Suite 320
Herndon, VA 20170
info@mascotbooks.com

Library of Congress Control Number: 2020913260

CPSIA Code: PRT0121A
ISBN-13: 978-1-64307-292-0

Printed in the United States

Wiggly Worm

and Her Friends Recycle Organics

Lissa Landry

illustrated by **Nidholm**

Wiggly Worm is a Red Wiggler worm.
Red Wigglers love to eat up organic
stuff like food, grass, and leaves.
They are the planet's recyclers.

After the Red
Wigglers eat all of
the good organics,
they leave really
good food behind
for the soil. It is
called compost.

LANDFILL

Compost rocks the roots of the plants with good food for them to use to grow our food. Red Wigglers know organics are not trash and do not belong in a trash truck or landfill. Come, let's learn about Wiggly Worm, her friends, and organics!

Wiggly's farm is a working farm. There is always lots of work to do on her farm. Lots of worms live in Wiggly's house on the farm. She has four friends. Their names are Melba (she is the older, wiser worm), Sarah, Linda, and Megan.

Wiggly

Linda

They are younger worms, like Wiggly. Melba is the teacher. She makes sure the other worms are doing their jobs. Recycling organics into compost is an important job because we do not want to fill up our landfills with organics.

Melba

Megan

Sarah

There are five horses on Wiggly's farm. The rancher likes to give horse rides to the children in the neighborhood. After the children have fun riding the horses, the organics are recycled by Wiggly and her friends.

At night, the barn where the horses sleep is cleaned out, and all the bedding straw is delivered to Wiggly's house.

The ranch helper cuts the big lawn at Wiggly's farm once a week, and he brings all his grass clippings over to Wiggly's house, too. Grass is wet with water inside, so Wiggly and her friends like that.

Grass has lots of good nitrogen, a nutrient good for the dirt that helps other plants grow big and strong. All compost must have nitrogen in it.

Wiggly's farm also sells apples and peaches from their orchard, and all the old fruit goes to Wiggly's house, too.

Wiggly and her friends like to go to the schools to help teach the kids about recycling organics. Just like we recycle our paper, cardboard, plastic, and glass, can we recycle organics?

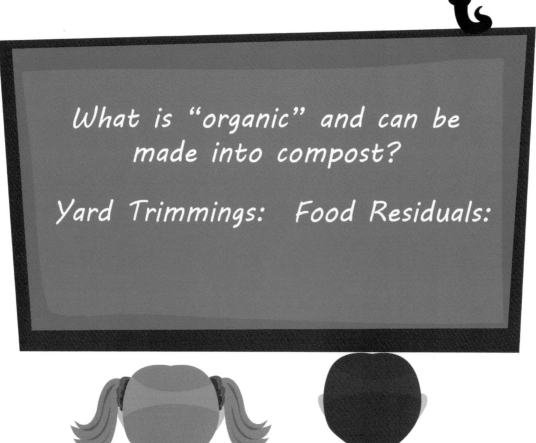

What is "organic" and can be made into compost?

Yard Trimmings: Food Residuals:

Mother Earth can re-use all the organics to grow the food, flowers, trees, and plants. Wiggly teaches the kids about what is organic.

Melba reminds Wiggly, Linda, Sarah, and Megan that there are many things that are organic. Organic means anything that will rot or decompose back into the dirt.

Melba and Wiggly know the organics do not belong in the landfill or in the trash can. It cannot be reused in a landfill.

Wiggly, Melba, Linda, and Sarah are all Red Wigglers who work hard every day to recycle organics. Can you find organics at your house and school that can be recycled?

Can you help Mother Earth to recycle organics too? Wiggly and her friends hope you will teach your friends to recycle organics.

What organics
can you recycle
at home?

There are over 10,000 species of worms.

Red Wiggler worms are the best worms for composting because...

* They love to eat! They can eat their body weight in food every day! Luckily, what's yucky to us is yummy to Red Wigglers. We can give our trash to them instead of throwing it away in a landfill.

* After they eat up your garbage, they produce something called *vermicompost,* which helps keep soil healthy.

* Some kinds of worms need to live deep under the soil, but Red Wigglers can live right beneath a layer of leaves or compost.

* They have so many nicknames! Scientists call them Eisenia foetida, but you can call them redworms, manure worms, brandling worms, and of course, Red Wigglers!

* They have a tiny flap over their mouths to filter food from soil and inedible debris. But, you can only see that flap with a microscope!

* They have five hearts and no eyes!

Things to feed a Red Wiggler:	Things NOT to feed a Red Wiggler:
Potato peels	Bones
Carrots	Meat (poultry + fish included)
Lettuce	Cheese
Cabbage	Butter
Celery	Salad dressings
Apple peels	Citrus
Non-citrus fruits	Mayonnaise/dairy
Crushed eggshells	Fried foods/oily foods
Coffee grounds (and filters)	Glossy paper
Cornmeal/oatmeal	
Tea bags	

About the Author

Lissa Landry is, first and foremost, a wife and mother of four grown children. Together with her family, she has owned and operated a composting company in Buellton, California for over thirty years. She is passionate about nature and teaching children about recycling organics with worms. Everything in nature has a purpose, and this has been her life's work.